SAGWA
The Chinese Siamese Cat

Bow Wow Meow

By George Daugherty and David Wong
Illustrations by Mel Grant and Chris George
Gretchen Schields, Creative Consultant

Based on the screenplay *Cha-Siu Bow Wow Miao*
written by George Daugherty and David Wong.
Illustrations based on storyboards by Lyne Hart.

Scholastic Inc.

New York   Toronto   London   Auckland   Sydney
Mexico City   New Delhi   Hong Kong   Buenos Aires

ISBN 0-439-45599-5

Sagwa, The Chinese Siamese Cat, is produced by CinéGroupe Sagwa Inc. in association with Sesame Workshop based on the book "The Chinese Siamese Cat" written by Amy Tan and illustrated by Gretchen Schields. © 2003 CinéGroupe Sagwa Inc. Characters and Original Story © 1994 Amy Tan. Illustrations © 1994 Gretchen Schields. "Sagwa" and its logo are trademarks of CinéGroupe Sagwa Inc. All rights reserved.

The "See it on PBS KIDS" logo is a trademark of the Public Broadcasting Service and is used with permission.

Published by Scholastic Inc. SCHOLASTIC and associated logos are trademarks and/or registered trademarks of Scholastic Inc.

12 11 10 9 8 7 6 5 4 3 2 1   3 4 5 6 7 8/0

Printed in the U.S.A.
First printing, November 2003

Sagwa, Dongwa, and Sheegwa were helping Mama Miao get ready
tomorrow's visit from their auntie Mei-Mei, uncle Miao, and cousin Cha-Siu.
ey were going to meet Cha-Siu for the first time, and the kittens were *really* excited.
"I can't wait," purred Sagwa.
"Neither can I," said Dongwa. "It'll be good to have another boy around. I can show
m my favorite tree."

"You can *all* have fun with Cha-Siu," said Mama. "It is so wonderful that your aunt and uncle have adopted him."

"Adopted?" said Sheegwa. "What's that mean?"

Mama explained that something had happened to Cha-Siu's parents when he was very young, so Auntie Mei-Mei and Uncle Miao had adopted him. "They are his parents now, and he's their son," she said.

The morning came, and before the kittens knew it, they were greeting their aunt and uncle.

"Where's Cha-Siu?" asked Dongwa.

Suddenly, there was a blur and a clatter as Cha-Siu raced by and then screeched a stop in front of them. When the dust settled, the kittens' jaws dropped in surprise.

"WOOF!" barked Cha-Siu. "Woof woof WOOF! Meooowwwwwww!"

"He's a *dog*!" whispered Sagwa.

"Who acts like a *cat*!" finished Dongwa.

Cha-Siu was so excited to meet his cousins that he ran around in circles, alm
catching his own tail. One moment, he would run around like a dog and bark and
his tail. And the next, he would meow like a cat. The kittens watched in amazeme

It was all very confusing to the kittens. That night, they went to talk to their mama.

"What's up with Cha-Siu?" Dongwa asked.

"Well, he's a little different from you," said Mama.

"He's a *puppy*!" exclaimed Sheegwa.

"And he can't be our cousin if he's a dog!" said Sagwa.

"Of course he's your cousin!" Mama said kindly.

"What you *look* like doesn't always determine who you are."

The kittens thought about what Mama had said.

"Even though he *is* a dog, Cha-Siu is a member of our family," continued Mama.

Sagwa and Sheegwa smiled. But Dongwa wasn't convinced.

"Do you understand, Dongwa?" asked Mama.

"Yes, Mama," said Dongwa. "Tomorrow we'll try to have fun."

Sagwa jumped in. "No, Dongwa. Tomorrow we *will* have fun!"

"Good girl, Sagwa," said Mama.

The next day, Cha-Siu was playing with his cousins, sometimes barking like a dog, other times meowing like a cat. He didn't seem to be confused at all.

"It's so great to have cousins!" said Cha-Siu.

"Yes," agreed Sheegwa and Sagwa, "this is *great!*"

"Yeah, great," mumbled Dongwa unenthusiastically.

Cha-Sui could do everything the kittens could do, or *almost* everything. When they got to Dongwa's favorite tree, the kittens climbed right up. But Cha-Siu couldn't climb. He jumped. He ran. He tried every possible way to get into the tree. But climbing trees is one thing a dog *can't* do, no matter how hard he tries.

Dongwa was disappointed.
"I'll try again!" said Cha-Siu. "I can do it!"
"Just forget it," said Dongwa.
Sagwa pulled her brother aside and asked
him what was wrong.

"Cha-Siu can't even climb a tree! I don't feel like playing anymore," said Dongwa. And he sulked off.

Cha-Siu was puzzled. "Where's Dongwa going?" he asked.

"Oh, he's not feeling very well," Sagwa said quickly. Cha-Siu looked disappointed. But he went off to the pond with Sagwa and Sheegwa.

There they found the three Sleeve Dogs, Ping, Pang, and Pong. Sagwa introduced her cousin. The three little dogs circled Cha-Siu, sniffing and snarling.

"Your *cousin?*" snarled Ping.

"He's a *dog!*" growled Pang.

"I *am* their cousin!" insisted Cha-Siu. "I'm a member of the Miao family! Meow! Meeeooowwwww WOOF WOOF!"

The Sleeve Dogs rolled on the ground, laughing.

"If you're a member of the Miao family," snarled Ping, "then climb that tree over there."

Cha-Siu froze in his tracks. He knew he couldn't climb a tree.

"A dog," Pong sneered, "who thinks he's part of a cat family!" The three dogs laughed and laughed and laughed.

Suddenly, a new voice interrupted all the laughing.

"Hey! Cut it out!" It was ongwa. He hadn't gotten ery far when he heard the eeve Dogs making fun of Cha-Siu. ongwa realized that Cha-Siu *was* part of s family and needed Dongwa's help.

Cha-Siu's eyes brightened with surprise.

"Quit messing with my cousin!" said ongwa. "He's a Miao — just like me!"

But the Sleeve Dogs were not so easily convinced.
"Let him prove it," snarled Ping.
"Yup, let's see him climb that tree," growled Pang.

Dongwa went over to Cha-Siu.
"OK, cuz. It's time to climb a tree,"
he said to the nervous puppy.

"But Dongwa, you *know* I can't climb
a tree!" whispered Cha-Siu.

"Sure you can," said Dongwa. "Your cousins are
here to help. Sagwa! Sheegwa! Over here!"

The two sisters scampered over to their brother.

"We can help Cha-Siu by doing the stair-step trick we learned from those acrobats!" Dongwa explained to his sisters.

"Hey, Sleeve Dogs," yelled Dongwa, "watch THIS!"

And just like Chinese acrobats,
the kittens flipped into formation,
making a feline stair step right up
to the lowest branch of the tree!

Cha-Siu knew just what to do. He walked up the kittens' "staircase" and sat down on a big branch of the tree. His three cousins then climbed up and sat beside him on the branch.

Dongwa looked down
the Sleeve Dogs.
"Did you see that? He
imbed the tree! And if you
er mess around with my
ousin again," he continued,
ou'll have *me* to deal with!
eoowwwww!"
The Sleeve Dogs yipped and
apped, then scampered off.

The four cousins laughed and giggled. Cha-Siu let out a bi
loud doggy "WOOF!!!" Then he covered his mouth, embarrassed
  "Hey, Cha-Siu, don't worry about it," said Dongwa. "W
think your 'woof' is really cool. Can you teach us how to do it?

Cha-Siu smiled a very big smile.
No problem. You just go like
is . . . WOOF!"
"Woof! Woof! Woof-woof!"
rked the kittens.

And there they all sat, on the branch of the tree. Three kittens and one puppy — all one family, woofing with delight!